dedicated to

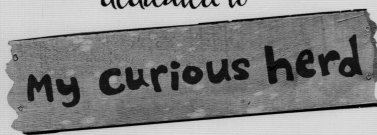

My curious herd

STERLING CHILDREN'S BOOKS
New York

An Imprint of Sterling Publishing Co., Inc.
1166 Avenue of the Americas
New York, NY 10036

ISBN 978-1-4549-2232-2

Distributed in Canada by Sterling Publishing Co., Inc.
c/o Canadian Manda Group, 664 Annette Street
Toronto, Ontario, Canada M6S 2C8
Distributed in the United Kingdom by GMC Distribution Services
Castle Place, 166 High Street, Lewes, East Sussex, England BN7 1XU
Distributed in Australia by NewSouth Books
45 Beach Street, Coogee, NSW 2034, Australia

For information about custom editions, special sales, and premium and corporate purchases, please contact Sterling Special Sales at 800-805-5489 or specialsales@sterlingpublishing.com.

Manufactured in China
Lot #:
10 9 8 7 6 5 4 3 2 1
06/17

www.sterlingpublishing.com

Illustrations were created digitally.
Design by Irene Vandervoort

PONY in the CITY

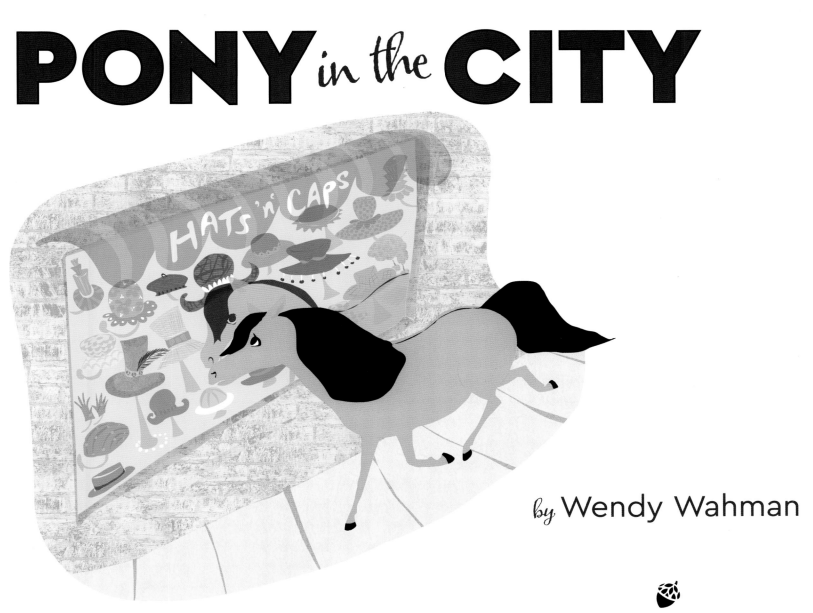

by Wendy Wahman

STERLING CHILDREN'S BOOKS
New York

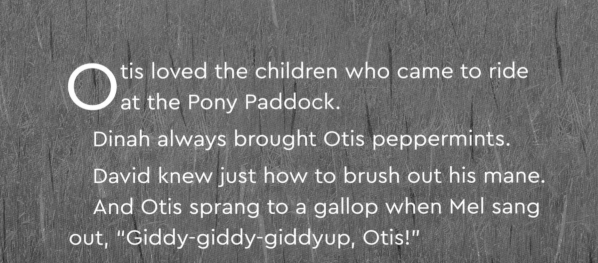

Otis loved the children who came to ride at the Pony Paddock.

Dinah always brought Otis peppermints.

David knew just how to brush out his mane. And Otis sprang to a gallop when Mel sang out, "Giddy-giddy-giddyup, Otis!"

Otis wanted to know all about the children.
"Do they gallop and kick?
Do they nicker and neigh?
Do they ever walk on all fours?"

All day long, so many questions!
The older ponies ignored Otis.
They flicked their tails.
They snorted.
They stamped their hooves and
whinnied.

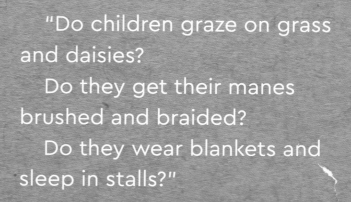

"Do children graze on grass
and daisies?

Do they get their manes
brushed and braided?

Do they wear blankets and
sleep in stalls?"

Otis

Mosey

Whinny

Derby

All night long, so many questions!
   The older ponies ignored Otis.
   They flicked their tails.
   They snorted.
   They stamped their hooves and whinnied,
"Go to sleep, Otis!"

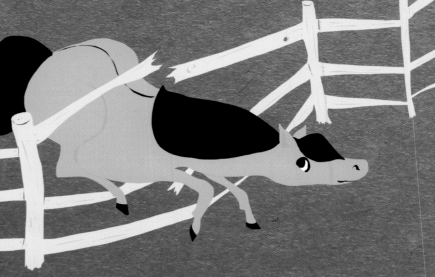

But Otis was saddled with questions.
So he went to find answers.

Clippity, clippity.
"Where do they keep the children?"
Cloppity, cloppity.
"In a barn? Out to pasture?"

"There they are!"
So many children!

Galloping and kicking.
Nickering and neighing.
Some children were even
walking on all fours.

Clippity, clippity.
"Oh! Children live in such
big barns."
Cloppity, cloppity.

"Whoa! Children *do* graze on grass and daisies."

"Say-hay-hay! Children *do* get brushed—and their manes braided."

"Children *do* wear blankets and sleep standing up in their stalls."

Otis yawned. He wished he was back home in the barn, tucked under his blanket, too.

Clippity, clippity.
So far from home!

Cloppity, cloppity,
So long since supper!

Clippity, clippity.
"Mosey?"
Cloppity, cloppity.
"Derby? Whinny?"

"Neigh hay-hay!
Dinah!
David!
Mel!"

The children led Otis home
with a song:

"Giddy-giddy-giddyup,
Otis!"
Clippity, clippity!
Cloppity, cloppity!

Otis yawned again. He couldn't wait to hit the hay.

First the children fed him carrots and oats.

Then they curried and combed him.

At last, they tucked him under his blanket.

But there was no sleep for Otis.
The older ponies flicked their tails.
They snorted.
They stamped their hooves and whinnied.

"Do children nicker and neigh?"
"Do they graze on grass and daisies?"
"Do they wear blankets and sleep in stalls?"

So many questions!
But Otis loved the other ponies.
So . . .

He answered all their
questions, one by one.

And then some.